Wednesday's Writer II

A Second Anthology

from the

Todmorden Writers' Group

Winter 2011

Compiled and Edited by Andy Fraser

ISBN: 978-1-4709-4885-6

Published via Lulu.com

1st Edition Printed 2011

Contents

Introduction

By *Andy Fraser*

The Todmorden Writers' Group has now been going four years. When I set it up with a small group of like-minded people back in 2007 I worried that there would not be enough creative writers in a town the size of Todmorden, especially with two other groups already doing the same thing. My sole selling point was an evening schedule to cater for those who worked during the day and enjoyed a relaxing drink with their writing.

I needn't have worried at all. Todmorden is awash with talented, bright and imaginative people of all ages and backgrounds, many of whom love to write. In the last four years the numbers attending the group have fluctuated, but the overall trend seems to be on the increase. Our highest point was a year ago when fourteen people attended one group meeting – a little hectic it must be said. We still have regular meetings of nine or ten and a membership currently standing at nineteen, which is very healthy and more than I could have imagined when I set it up.

So, with all this talent at our fingertips, putting together an anthology should be a simple matter, you might think? Well, think again. In the year since the last anthology was published, the group have written around 150 stories, poems and scripts, from sixteen members. To whittle these down to only eighteen entries has been very difficult indeed. Each piece was voted on democratically by all members and I hope the resulting mix of poetry and prose will have something for every reader and a good balance of emotion and thought, action and reaction. I would say that the overall feel of this year's anthology is darker though not in a sinister way. There is more about loss and sadness, more about the everyday grind that is life and love, and I suppose this is only to be expected in the current political and economic climate.

Where competitions are concerned the group have had some successes and some failures in the last year but just as I send this book to press, it has been announced that Elizabeth McLaughlin, who here presents *To My Darling Mary*, and is quite a new recruit to the writers' group, was voted overall winner in the Voices of Todmorden monologue writing competition. Well done Liz! It also means that the Todmorden Writers' Group holds onto its crown as the overall winner of the previous competition was Alison Shelton, who has a couple of pieces in this anthology.

If you live in or around Todmorden and you would like to become part of a passionate, varied and above all friendly writers' group, the door is always open. Please drop me an email to fraserai@yahoo.com and I will get back in touch as soon as possible.

Andy Fraser

Superpower

John Clarke

Superpower

by *John Clarke*

I come here to speak a poetry older than your own
I come with you into my house as a lost brother
I come to stand in the sun at the end of a day's tilling
I come to face south-west and be silent
I come to give the world another vision

You come with a physique not earned through a tilling of
the earth
You come with surprise that my skin is as light as your own,
my eyes as green
You come with sweets thrown to the children
You come with cameras to capture the children's eyes
You come with vehicles to run down the children

I am the one you have chosen
I am to fall amidst a day's tilling
I am to be photographed as animal kill
I am to be tied to another who too is not buried
I am to be dismembered amidst the dust

You are flying west with no call to prayer
You are standing with a medal as bright as the sun
You are looking into the green eyes of your brother and not
thinking
You are standing in the sun at the end of a day's drinking
You are telling your children at dusk a story of Babylon

The Perfect Day

Peter Baber

The Perfect Day

by *Peter Baber*

"It's odd, when you think about it," he said.

"What is?" she said.

"The allusion – reference, sorry – to drinking Sangria in the park. It must mean the song's about something that actually happened."

"Why?" she asked, genuinely looking puzzled.

"Oh come on," he said, wrinkling up his nose in that endearing way she remembered. "No one really drinks Sangria in the park. Not in England, anyway. So if you were going to write what I guess is a song about a romantic day out, you wouldn't talk about Sangria. You might mention – I don't know – Pimms, say, or Chardon-"

"I would," she said. "I mean I think I may once have. Drank Sangria in the park. With someone. I can't remember who."

She was trying to remember how they had got onto this subject. She hoped she hadn't encouraged him.

As she wondered she let a wisp of her hair fall down across her cheek. She sucked in the end of it as she breathed.

He remembered that was one of her habits he had found most appealing when he had first known her all those years ago. It was good to see things hadn't changed.

"Do you," he said, "remember the times we spent in parks when we were students? When we still thought – or perhaps I did – that we could change the world and everything."

"Did I go to the park with you?" she asked, tracing the railing she was holding with a foot clad in an expensive pair of docksiders. "I don't remember."

He was pained, scandalised. Could she really not remember those times, usually on a summer afternoon but once or twice in the first light of dawn, after staying up all night discussing whether you could really take Simone de Beauvoir seriously?

He coughed. "I think we may have done," he said. Could she not remember? Sometimes she would just run out barefoot, and he remembered best of all the time he had impaled his coat jacket on a railing spike trying to lift her over to get in early one morning to the private gardens they weren't really allowed in. She had giggled wildly and hid behind a hedge as they heard someone approaching. He had just got away in time, but only by tearing the sleeve of his jacket which had been his grandfather's.

Such memories were the reason why he had suggested meeting here in this park, although it was different from the one where they had been before. That was across the city, back near the college where he had taken his degree, and was difficult to get to from the institution where he worked now. He realised this was now his third academic position, all as it happened in the same northern city. Five years so far of tutoring mostly bored teenagers, and then working late into the night to bring out a new paper that was wildly applauded and forgotten. And in all that time not a word from her, not since he had returned after his viva to find a note saying she was finally off for the last time, but would keep in touch. Then nothing until last Thursday afternoon. He had been finishing off a Pot Noodle in his office, feeling sweaty after a rare visit to the college's gym, when suddenly a message popped into his inbox. How had she got his address? She must have Googled him. "Hiyeee," it said. "Remember me? I know it's been a long time, but I happen to be in town this weekend at a loose end (don't ask) and wondered if you fancied meeting up?"

He had felt the years collapsing as he rang the number she had given and left a voicemail suggesting they meet here.

"Actually I do remember the park," she was saying, "with loads of people. The girls, of course, and Chris and Rob. Oh and Ian, obviously. But you? I can't recall."

He sighed to himself. He could, of course, remember all the people she mentioned even though he had not seen any of them for at least as long as he had not seen her, if not longer. The girls were a group of chatty women, all of whom he secretly thought were beneath her intellectually. One or two had even gone into nursing after finishing their degrees. Chris and Rob were two mechanical engineering students she had picked up at a party somewhere who she occasionally invited around to her rooms "for a bit of variety". He had always found them stupid, partly because they only ever seemed to be interested in what her breasts looked like for real. They even asked him, as if he knew. Once, after a particularly long and heavy night, she had let them find out.

And then there was Ian. Ian the boyfriend she had had right through college, Ian who she had met at a party her parents had given, who had taken her to New York for the first time. "He's got a terribly important position," she said, "in the bank. He's always shooting off to meet really important people."

He noticed that she never seemed interested in meeting these important people herself. Ian it was who regularly used to turn up at a moment's notice. She would drop everything, fly into his arms, and then not be seen for days until she would appear again, brandishing a bottle that was just too expensive for her. Of course he let her in.

He remembered one time Ian had arrived and they had departed, then suddenly half an hour later Ian was back knocking on his door. "Sorry mate," he said. "You wouldn't have any hot chocolate, would you? Turns out she wants one. You know what she's like." Only now did he wonder why Ian was never jealous of him.

He had heard at a party that Ian and her might have parted, were no more. But he didn't dare hope.

An awkward passage gathered between them as they now started walking. But she filled it. "Do you know," she said, "talking about that song just makes me shiver at what I used to do. The stuff you and I used to listen to. Do you remember that other Lou Reed album you made me buy? The one with the kids really crying in it? Dear God what a load of rubbish." And she really did shiver.

"Berlin," he said, matter-of-factly. "Released in the wake of Transformer. But never really lived up to that album's potential. Stalled really."

He was aware he was going on, but could not stop himself.

"But I do like Transformer. Especially Perfect Day, as you know. I even quite liked that naff charity version of it they brought out a few years ago. You know, the one where David Bowie is one of the singers. That must have been weird for him because he was the producer of the original record. It's like when China Girl came out. Everyone said his version of it was a rubbish cover version of the Iggy Pop original, but I don't see how you call it a cover version because he co-wrote the song."

She was looking at him blankly.

"I'm sorry," he said. "I know I go on sometimes."

But now she was smiling under her fringe.

"I've just remembered that's what I loved about you," she said. "All those silly facts and figures you used to spout out. It used to keep me entertained. Look, why don't we sit for a while over there?"

And he followed her sheepishly to a park bench where she sat down and pulled up her coat collar. For it was a cold November day.

They started talking and soon found they had much to talk about. The years might have passed, but the films they had watched and the books they had read to while away the listless hours had been remarkably similar. The more she talked, the more he found himself slipping back to how it had been back then, when talking to her, if that was all it was, had still seemed part of nature.

They found out that only a year ago they had narrowly missed bumping into each other in a Las Vegas hotel where they had both been staying – he on a conference, she on well-earned corporate hospitality spree. That made them laugh, and talk on.

Presently she said she was hungry and felt like lunch. "We could go in there," she said, pointing behind where they sat. Over the railings he could see a small Italian restaurant. "It looks fine," he said.

He didn't want to tell her that he had spent the previous evening scouring the web for a suitable restaurant to wow her with, and had found one apparently near here, a Tunisian establishment, not Moroccan that everyone went to now, and heavily rated. He had taken down the address and had even arrived slightly before their meeting today to check it out. But damn it if there weren't any street signs around here.

This Italian was as he had expected. Heavy wooden Venetian blinds made it feel like the evening in the middle of the day, and airbrushed pictures of men on Vespas got you in the mood for feeling you were in Italy, even if the food wasn't really there.

They were halfway through lunch when he finally decided to ask her. "Are you still with him?" he said.

"Who, Ian? No – God no", she said, gulping down her wine. "We split, not long after college ended. He was always away in New York, and I was busy here, and I kind of suspected. Anyway, things didn't work out. I think he's married now. With two kids. It was so what he wanted."

The waiter arrived with desert – she had chosen a particularly creamy meringue concoction. While she studied it, he felt the pleasant but nervous sensation of rising expectation. Suddenly she said: "Do you know what the worst thing about Ian was?"

"No." Several things sprung to mind. "I couldn't possibly say."

She took her first bite of the meringue. "It was the sex," she said. "Ooh the sex. It was ghastly. He always used to demand it as soon as he turned up on those late nights. He would jump on me as soon as we'd closed the door in a way that was supposed to be romantic but I just thought was boring. He explained it was necessary relief after a hard day. Yet when I ever actually felt like it and he didn't he would just lie there simpering at me. That's when I noticed how fat he was getting. As for technique – well, straight in and out. I could have had more fun with a loofah. At least it would have stayed stiff."

He laughed nervously.

"I am sorry," she continued, "but I really feel you're someone I can actually tell these things. You know, you're understanding."

"And Ian wasn't?" he asked.

"No," she said quickly. "In fact the last times he turned up at university, I said I was too busy for more than a coffee. I blamed it on my dissertation. You know, the one you more or less ended up writing for me in the end."

"Oh no, I don't really," he chuckled. But didn't say much else, because by now a new and superior form of excitement was taking him over. One that he had rarely, experienced before. It wasn't just the wine. Oh, how well this was progressing. Ian had been conquered, despatched with, forgotten. If only he had known back then. And now, as the afternoon stretched before them, she seemed his.

"So," he said as he quietly paid the bill. "What shall we do now?"

How annoying, but typical, that at just such a moment that song came back to him. They could feed animals in the zoo, perhaps, he laughed to himself. Then maybe a movie too and then home. Home was currently a couple of rooms in a hall he had agreed to become warden of to earn a bit of money. But would she mind that?

He suddenly noticed she was looking at her watch. It was one of those skimpy feminine ones.

"Oh gosh, is that the time?" she said. "It's already four! Look, I'm really sorry but I've got to go. My boyfriend will be waiting for me."

Shards of ice hit him, so hard he actually gulped. He hoped she hadn't seen. "Your boyfriend?" he said. "You didn't tell me."

"Oh yes," she said, trying to raise her voice above an ambulance that blared past the window. "I met Greg through a friend of Ian's. It's down to him that I'm down up here this weekend at all. He's got some sort of sales conference – they do try to come out to the regions - and it's strictly no partners. But he wants to get out of it as soon as possible. He wants us to go back home tomorrow so we can carry on doing up the flat.

"The flat," he said. "Yes, I see."

"Because we're going off to Barbados for a fortnight the week after next. Oh, he'll already be waiting for me. He says he's always waiting for me. Says it's one of the sacrifices of his life."

She smiled weakly.

"So listen," she said, getting up, "I am sorry to have to leave you like this."

"It's nothing," he just got out. "Not at all."

"But I have enjoyed it. In fact, I was a bit nervous about this afternoon. But you know, I'm glad I spent it with you."

Then a quick peck on the cheek, that felt warm, and she was out through the swing doors.

He studied the picture of Elizabeth Fry on the fiver he was leaving as a tip. He still couldn't remember who she was.

Outside waiting for the tram – a new development since she had last been here – she sat down on a bench, wiped some fluff out of her hair, and started reading her new paperback.

But the story did not prove as exciting as she had hoped, and she found herself drifting off, letting the spine hit her knee.

The lunch hadn't actually proved as odd as she had feared. She never told anyone, but she actually hated being in a large city on her own. She found it frightening. She had only gone to college here because her parents were still living in the city. But they had since retired to France, and she found it unfamiliar.

So how extraordinary that just as she was heaving down a suitcase to get ready for this trip, she had also knocked down an old diary that happened to fall out at a page that mentioned him. It hadn't taken her long to track him down. She still kept an eye on who was where in academia. Just in case one day she might go back. You never knew.

And there was more. She remembered fondly now how much she enjoyed talking to him. She hadn't had that kind of serious-minded conversation in months. It made her feel – how did that phrase go? – someone new, someone good. Because, when she now came down to it, there were some things that were not good about her life with Greg. She really did not like the approach of this new company he had joined in what he assured her was the opportunity of a lifetime. It seemed all too pushy when all they were selling was a paltry bit of hardware put together in the Third World. She had actually lied back then when she had said that partners weren't invited. She just hadn't been able to bear the idea of an afternoon in the spa with the corporate wives.

She did wonder how he might have viewed the afternoon. Was he in love with her? It was hard to say. He had once been, definitely, and really embarrassingly, in their first year at college, bursting into her room with a new album he said she must listen to, when she was already with Ian. Why had she ever admitted to liking Lou Reed? But now? Well, maybe yes, maybe no. Anyway, she thought, as the tram finally squeaked up, every girl could possibly do with having a man in the background. It would never come to anything.

He, meanwhile, found himself heading to the franchise store that had recently opened across the street from his hall. The blast of warmth as he went in unsettled him, but he found the need to make even meagre choices – lasagne or salmon en-croute, Australian Chardonnay or Pinot Grigio – was a useful distraction. For what had happened this afternoon had happened so often before, and he was determined not to let it ruin the rest of the day. After all, he saw, picking up the Saturday paper, there was the final part of that TV drama tonight.

No, the time for recriminations would come when he was waking up the next morning in the same old functional room, the radiator ticking and a long, lonely Sunday ahead.

"You have a good evening now, won't you?" the African man at the checkout said. He grunted a reply, pitying him for the scratchy bright uniforms the franchise owner forced his staff to wear.

Outside a light drizzle made the pavement shiny. He walked carefully. Oh why did these situations always end up like this? Would he ever know? Turning the corner, he came across the usual Saturday afternoon crazy preacher. Even an oncoming winter was not stopping him from appearing. "And the lord says as he says to all people," he bawled, "as he said through the blessed St Paul: 'Whatsoever a man soweth, that shall he also reap.'"

He walked on, humming.

Charlie

Alison Shelton

Charlie

by *Alison Shelton*

Charlie hides in his head. At home he gets up, eats breakfast and goes to school, and sometimes he is naughty, but here there are lots of other people that he doesn't know, so he hides in his head. But it is alright because his teacher Kenney is here and some children from his class. There are lots of other children too, but Charlie doesn't know them so he ignores them completely and pretends they are not there.

Charlie has been having fun. He has been kayaking and climbing and has done archery. He got gold on archery which was really good and the teacher said he had done well, but Charlie didn't know that teacher so he just went inside for his tea instead.

But just now Charlie is crying. And Alison is giving him a hug, and a tissue for his bloody lip and wet eyes, and is rubbing his sore shin. Alison is not his teacher but she is friends with Kenny and she has been with Charlie all week so he is friends with her too. Charlie has fallen off his mountain bike, and they have only just set off. Alison says he has hurt the tree too and Charlie says I didn't mean to. And then Alison says it's all right Charlie, the tree is alright. And Charlie strokes the green dampness which was hiding under the tree bark that has been scraped off.

Alison says can you be brave and keep going. It would be a shame to go back now because you'll miss The Big Down Hill, but we will have to catch up with the others. So Charlie climbs back on his bike and peddles down the track between Alison and Kenny. Charlie's legs are going up and down really fast and Alison and Kenny's legs are going slow and steady, but it doesn't matter because the bikes are all going the same speed.

They catch up with the rest of the group and Alison says, you remember I told you about the Big Up Hill. This is the Big Up Hill so if you put number one on the left handlebar and number one on the right handle bar we can see how far up the Big Hill we can pedal. So Charlie and Alison pedal up the Big Up Hill and halfway up Charlie says that his leg is still hurting and he needs to walk instead. Alison says it's a good job because she was getting really tired and didn't think she could keep up with him. So they jump off the bikes and push them up the steep hill. Charlie's leg is still hurting so Alison asks him about playing Basketball, and Charlie tell her all about the teams that he plays for and how many baskets he has scored and how fast he is. He tells her all about Michael Jordan and how he has scored 32,392 baskets and won trophies in all the leagues. Alison asks if there are any good Basketball players in England, and Charlie says that there's no one as good as Charlie is and makes Alison laugh.

Then they are at the top and Charlie is disappointed because there is no Big Down Hill, but Alison tells him that they have to go down some small hills first to get practice in. Charlie races down the hills shouting at the top of his voice at the sky and at the others. Alison is right behind him saying well done Charlie! Then everyone stops. While they wait for the others to catch up, Alison says she must have chocolate flavour skin because the midges are eating her up. Charlie says that because his skin is brown, the midges must think he is chocolate flavoured too and that's why they are eating him up. The other teacher is telling them that this is the Big Down Hill and that they must be careful. Alison reminds Charlie that he needs to use his left brake to slow down. She asks him which is his left break and Charlie shows her.

Then they are off, and the wind is flying past and Charlie is yelling and Alison is yelling and the wheels are zooming around and Charlie is laughing and laughing when they get to the bottom. He says that the Big Down Hill was mint. Alison says that it was brilliant and that it's all the way back in to the minibus now for lunch, but Charlie says he wants to ride slowly. So they do and the rest of the group disappear off down the track in front of them. The sun is shining through the breaks in the trees so Charlie and Alison are light, dark, light, dark, light, dark. Alison says that she has heard Charlie is brilliant at singing Robbie Williams songs, so Charlie starts off singing and he and Alison ride along the track singing 'She's The One' in harmony.

On, off, on, off; the sunlight bursts on him like a camera flash.

And,
just for today,
Charlie is a Superstar.

A Mother's Strength

Cindy Shanks

A Mother's Strength

by *Cindy Shanks*

Silhouetted in the amber glow
Screams – a smouldering gun.
Salty tears, crimson flow.

Alone the silent noise echoes
I grasp the essence of my son
Silhouetted in the amber glow.

Blood pours too fast, time too slow.
Points scored. No one has won.
Salty tears, crimson flow.

In feverish prayer I cry in sorrow
As sirens wail, warm blood runs.
Silhouetted in the amber glow.

Hands pressing me to let go.
Meaningless words from everyone.
Salty tears crimson flow.

Strength inside begins to grow.
The fight within has begun.
Silhouetted in the amber glow.
Salty tears, crimson flow.

Doctor Faustus

Richard Holley

Doctor Faustus

by *Richard Holley*

"Are you really called Doctor Faustus?"

"Yes," John sighed as he looked outside. There was a poodle staring through the window at him, "That dog again," he thought to himself.

"John Faustus and you're a doctor?"

"It's Faust actually."

"Wah ha ha ha, did your parents actually give you the title of doctor when you born? Wah ha ha ha."

"A lot of patients claim that their GP doesn't take them seriously, but it works both ways," John thought to himself, "If he's just going to laugh at me I'm going to chuck him a placebo and look on Facebook." Facebook was John's guilty pleasure. He saw his profile as an alternate self, a homunculus that people were only ever nice to.

The phone rang.

"Dr John," he said into the receiver, preferring to avoid the connotations his surname held.

"Hi Doctor it's Nurse Helen." Just hearing her voice made John feel twenty years younger. "I'm with Mrs Hobbes, would you be able to fit her in after your next appointment?"

"You know me Helen, anything for my patients."

"You're such a sweetheart, thank you." Helen hung up the phone.

"She called me a sweetheart," John thought wistfully to himself, momentarily forgetting how irksome Mrs Hobbes could be; her ailments being at least as much of a torment to him as they were to her.

"Will you be along on Sunday Doctor?"

"I don't think it really does anything for me Mrs Hobbes."

"I know having your wife leave you must be hard, I never had a husband leave me, but I did have two that died, the church always was a great help."

John used to attend church with his wife, but the ceremonies were always meaningless to him: he never thought that he would start to feel that way about medicine though.

As Mrs Hobbes words grated like nails on a chalkboard a small figure jumped out of the computer screen.

"Isn't technology fascinating," Mrs Hobbs declared peering over the top of her glasses at the small humanoid creature.

"You can see that thing too?" John asked in disbelief.

"Of course I can," Mrs Hobbes' replied, "Is it an 'app' as they say, something to do with Facebook?"

"Yes," the humanoid said, "I am Doctor Faust's homunculus."

"Marvellous," Mrs Hobbes declared as she got up to leave. "By the way is that your dog outside?"

"It's been following me for days," John managed to say despite being almost completely transfixed on the homunculus. He gingerly grabbed the creature and hid it in his draw before his next patient came in.

At the end of the day John left the surgery with the homunculus in his briefcase. Standing outside he watched Helen walking away in the distance.

"Was this the face that launched a thousand ships and burnt the topless towers of Ilium?"

John turned around to look where the voice came from, but nobody was present except the poodle that kept following him. There was an explosion of smoke and the poodle transformed into a demon.

"Mephistopheles?" John asked.

"In person," the demon replied,

"Is it just because of my name?" John asked irritably.

"What? Oh, of course: Doctor Faustus, ha ha."

"Humph, even The Devil, takes the piss out of me," John grumbled under his breath.

"Coincidence I assure you. Now Fau... erm John, ahem; sign your soul over to me and I will serve you with all my power for twenty years. Of course afterwards you will come to serve me."

John signed the contract without hesitation, slightly to the surprise of Mephistopheles.

"So where do want to start? That beautiful nurse; you want to be with her don't you?"

"More than anything in the world," John said gazing after her.

Mephistophiles summoned a clone of Helen who approached John and smiled lovingly at him. John raised a hand to her cheek but stopped himself from making contact and looked away.

"She's not real is she?" John said.

"Does it matter?"

"Yes. Yes it matters."

"Humph," Mephistophiles grunted. He then clicked his fingers and the two of them were transported instantly to the outside of Helen's house. Helen pulled up in her car and stepped out.

"John," she exclaimed. She ran up to the doctor and flung her arms around his neck.

John gently removed her arms and stared at her in desperation. "You're controlling her mind," he said.

"I thought you wanted her."

"Not like this."

Mephistopheles didn't understand John's remaining moral conviction as his soul was no longer able to be saved. Though he thought it better not to dwell on the matter.

"What about this then?" Mephistopheles suggested, growing slightly impatient. He raised his hand and the sky cleared of clouds, the sun shone brightly and plant life sprang up all around.

"Yes I like that, could I have that ability?" John asked eagerly.

Mephistopheles was pleased that John was finally showing some interest, but a little concerned when he used the ability to bring rain and create ugly grey buildings.

John wasn't interested in being granted any other abilities but he nonetheless attracted the interest of millions of people when they found out what he could do: at least at first. As the years passed people's fascination gave way to frustration and boredom because as soon as John got talking he always started going on about the girl who got away and the more he droned on and on, the more miserable the weather became. Everywhere he went he truly took the weather with him; it spread for hundreds of miles and made him extremely unpopular. He never actually caused any harm so nothing could really be done about him. Eventually the government came to an agreement with the homunculus, who acted as a sort of PR agent for John, that he and Faust could have a vast expanse of land and live unmolested as long as John stayed away from civilisation. The homunculus also maintained John's Facebook profile.

20 years passed and John's contracted time was almost up. His powers were fading and people across the country celebrated as the weather brightened with John's approaching death. An angel appeared before him to encourage him in the knowledge that his soul could still be saved. John was phlegmatic to say the least, but he seemed to display a vague sign of interest in the idea of salvation. John was then visited by a dark angel.

"Thou wretch Faustus thou art damned, beware lest thou bring forward the time when the torments of Hell fall upon thee," The dark angel bellowed. Mephistopheles coughed into his hand and beckoned the dark angel over to him.

"Leave him to repent," Mephistopheles said.

"Have you lost your sense of purpose?" The angel asked.

"I grant people their dreams so I can have the satisfaction of seeing their despair when I take them away. I've followed this miserable wretch for twenty years and never once has he displayed the slightest hint of pleasure or excitement. To be honest, being around him is downright depressing. I can't bear the thought of his company any longer, let alone for an eternity, whether he is serving me or not."

"Hmm you might have a point there, but I don't think a contract has ever been rescinded before, can it even be done?"

"If you wish it to be so," the voice was of an old man who had just entered the room.

"In the name of Heaven and Hell and all that is false or true in the universe, I wish it to be so."

"Then it is done," the old man said, "John you are free of your obligations to this demon."

"Never again," Mephistopheles grumbled as he stepped into a portal to the underworld.

John closed his eyes as the rain ceased, the clouds disappeared and the sun beamed brightly overhead. Mephistopheles gave up condemning souls when he discovered he could have more fun tormenting people as a health and safety inspector. As for the homunculus, well, with his duty done to John, he earned tremendous renown in the public eye and became a major reality television star.

John sat up, his magical powers had gone but his physical strength had returned. "Am I not dying?" he asked the old man who observed him sympathetically.

"In a sense I suppose we are all dying."

"But I'm not going to die today?"

"Oh I think you've got a good few years left in you yet Doctor."

"Maybe my remaining years would be better suited to someone else, someone leaving behind a life that is actually worthwhile."

"Don't be so eager to write life off my friend, you might be surprised at what we can sometimes find when the sands of time are given the chance to run off a little." The old man left John's house but as it was the first sunny day in a long time, he left the door open for the light to shine in.

With such an uncertain destiny and now alone, John felt at a loss as to what to do. He heard footsteps in the kitchen.

"Have you got any ideas?" John called out, thinking it was the old man.

"The door was open... I don't know if you remember me... we used to work together." John had been in the presence of angels but the sight before him was so beautiful as to make him certain that even God must have dreams.

"H...Helen."

"It wasn't easy to find you, I was worried that it might be too late, that I might never..." Helen was older but John observed in her a certain reserve and depth, an experience of life which made him feel closer to her, yet he was still speechless in her presence. Helen continued, "I saw Mrs Hobbes before she passed away recently. She was wilier than anyone gave her credit."

"Mrs Hobbes," John chuckled in reminiscence.

"She said she always asked me to make her appointments with you because she knew you'd do anything for me... was that true?"

"Yes."

"And the rain that followed you everywhere, people said it was because you were in love with someone, who was it?"

"It was you Helen, it was always you."

"Oh John, why did you never say anything?"

"You are happily married, you would either have felt nothing or felt bad. It would have served only my own gratification."

"I *was* married. Troy and I... when we were young it was like we were made for each other... there was never anything nasty, we just grew apart." There was silence between them for a few moments. "Your homunculus has left you alone like me... I thought that maybe, if you wanted, you might like to have some company?"

"Helen I..." John was so happy he could barely speak. Helen threw her arms around him and held him tightly as they kissed - the first of many. While they had missed out on 20 years together, that knowledge enabled them to make the most of their remaining long life, every moment of which was spent in true happiness.

Still Jim

Christine Potter

Still Jim

by *Christine Potter*

he was 'still Jim' sometimes
'how are you' he'd say, 'have a cup of tea'
but mostly 'not Jim' turned up for visitors
whose names he had forgotten, mealtimes
he couldn't remember, food he didn't eat

'not Jim' left his shirt unbuttoned
his beloved pomade abandoned, his hair
no longer sleek. Words tangled before his eyes
and were lost, like his love of jokes
his cash, his glasses or worst of all, his teeth

'still Jim' glimpsed occasionally like a dust mote
caught in sunlight or a half-remembered tune
whose title is lost, brought false hope
and memories of him whole and well
'safe home now' he'd say 'ring when you get back'

using up his stock of phrases he'd start again
with a stuttering intermittent reception
blinking in and out of the scribble that was his life
and we prayed for 'still Jim' to be there
hoping he could recapture what we had lost

he shrank before our eyes, his step faltered
his bruises darkened as 'not Jim' took control
but at his Requiem the Advent wreath caught fire
on the altar, and we wanted to laugh as he would have
'still Jim' had come back to us

Beneath the Stone

Andy Fraser

Beneath the Stone

by *Andy Fraser*

The world clings. So close that sounds get lost, squeezed, smothered in the surrounding water that presses hard against my eardrums. I hear my heart loud inside me, not beating but whooshing with fluid. When I open my eyes I can see the sun, bouncing and breaking above me through the lens of distressed liquid; thousands of tiny bubbles, journeying purposefully towards the light as I fall with equal determination to the darkness below. And on my shoulders, strapped to me with chains and knots beyond my ability to untie, sits the stone - its weight pulling me down, its uneven surface cold against my skin, as cold as death itself. I breathe and watch the bubbles dance away. The last struggle of life departing and I begin to gulp in the water, ever-more greedily in shorter and shorter starts until I am only sipping at the ocean depths in darkness. The sun is long gone.

I wake up and it is dark even with my eyes open. The muffled sounds of the sea are replaced by the coarse snoring of my husband beside me. I look at the clock, shining red through the black. 05:34. It will be light in less than an hour but I have no intention of returning to my dreams. I reach the light and turn it on then gently swing my legs out of bed without disturbing the duvet or George. It is not cold but as I open the door I pick up my dressing gown and wrap it around me for security. The bathroom light is on. One of the boys must have left it on when they went to bed. I understand that each generation needs to rebel against their parents but what type of rebellion includes leaving lights on, lids off or doors open after them?

I go to the loo and wash my hands. Ostensibly I wash them to clean them. Really it is a ruse to let me stare at myself in the mirror. The hair, greying and flat, forehead lined like old decking, eyes like counter-sunk holes in sallow cheeks, mouth thin and down-turned with wrinkles radiating from the lips not from smoking but years of disapproval. I realise the light is unflattering and my face still needs time to smooth out the night time creases … and yet I don't recognise the woman in the mirror at all. Not in the slightest. There is nothing of the woman I was, nothing even of the woman I hoped to be. I feel a tear spring into my eyes so I splash myself with water and tell myself to get a grip.

Downstairs there is the inevitable tidy and washing up to do. Ben is nineteen and Ian is nearly eighteen so they're bound to make a bit of a mess when they come in. George and I were in bed when they got home last night but I lay awake listening as they offered their friends wine from George's rack and food from the freezer. I mentally counted the plates, the pots and pans, the glasses and calculated how much mess they would leave and how long it would take me to tidy away before breakfast. I smile with some satisfaction as I run a sink of water. I am not off by much.

Once the dishes are done and away I sit down in front of the television with a cup of tea. The next thing I know George is shouting down the stairs. 'Annabelle, have you seen my grey shirt? The one with the cufflinks?'

I don't mind that by "have you seen" he means "have you washed". I don't mind that he hasn't even looked in the wardrobe where I told him I had hung it yesterday; washed and ironed. What I do mind is that he calls me Annabelle. That really tears at my heart. It's stupid, I know. Why shouldn't he call me Annabelle? It is my name. It's just not his name for me. It's not 'Belle' or 'Bella'. I've not heard those names for a long time. Even terms like 'darling' and 'dearest' now sound patronising and impatient when they leave his mouth.

"In the wardrobe." I call up to him.

"Ah, yes. Found it." No apology, no thank you. I take my empty cup to the sink and wash it before turning my attention to breakfast.

The next hour is a blur. Motion, colour, energy. George and the boys are up, cleaning and preening, dressing and stressing as they prepare for work or college. They fly past, twirling, firing questions at me: Where? When? Have I? Then they slide away, gracefully. They dance their way through the breakfast I have made them, despite having only four eggs, thanks to the boys' midnight sandwiches. My plate is the one that remains obstinately empty and unremarked.

"Hey mum. Ben and I are going to see a gig at the Riverside tonight. Can you drop us there at, like, 8?"

I look to George. "Sorry but your dad and I are going out tonight."

He looks up from breakfast television. "Are we?"

"Yes, we're going over to Stewart and Lindsay's for a meal."

Ian throws himself back in his chair and snarls through a curtain of lank hair. "Oh, Mum! We've bought tickets and everything."

"Well, maybe you should have checked with us first."

"How were we to know? You never go out."

"Not often, no. So we're going to enjoy ourselves tonight."

"Actually, tonight's not so good." It's George. He doesn't look at me while he says it. He doesn't watch the television either. His gaze flits like a bat around the room, never stopping, never landing near me even for a second. "We've got a new production team coming in and I sort of ... You should have told me."

"I did tell you George, twice. I even wrote it on the fridge."

"Well, I'll try and get away early. Tell you what, if you take the boys down to the Riverside and I'll try to get back for 8:30 or so, we can go to Stewart's-"

"They said 7. We can't turn up two hours late. They're cooking. It'll be ruined."

"I'll see what I can do." George finally looks at me and his eyes are as cold as any stone - without compassion, without love; only the haunted look of sacrifice, of compromise of one who begrudges his life. I hate him for that look. I take his plate from the table and scrape the detritus into the bin.

Chairs scrape and the dance of life picks up from where it left off. The boys tango with passion, George presents a wary pasodoble around me while I stand leaden and clumsy in his presence. I can only watch as their personal bubbles shimmy and slide up toward the light. Then they are gone and I am left with the plates and cups and washing up and a dirty bathroom awash with towels. Maybe it's the lack of sleep that does it. It could be. I lay in bed for an age last night listening to Ben and Ian until they turned in and by that point George was snoring. I can't sleep once he gets going so I lay there looking at the shadows on the ceiling, my arms clamping the duvet close to my body, pinning me in. I can stay like that for hours. So, maybe it's because I'm tired, that's why I don't start the cleaning immediately, but sit on the sofa and just cry and cry and cry. Huge wailing sobs that I can't control, that drown me in tears, that choke my chest, forcing me to snatch at what little air is present in the vacuum of my life.

Sometimes I struggle. Sometimes I glimpse the sun through the water and I know that if I could only reach it, feel its warmth on my face and breathe in the air that surrounds it I will be fine. I pull at the straps, the chains, the knots that I barely remember tying, back in the days when the boulder was small and light and didn't feel like a burden at all.

Other times the struggle seems too much, the sun too far away, the water too cold and I just let myself go. I watch the bubbles rise into the light until I can produce no more and the darkness closes in over my head. I still hear the screams, from inside, but they are from someone else, someone I knew long ago.

After an hour or so I dry my eyes and begin the washing up.

We Few, We Few

We Band of Brothers

Cindy Shanks

We Few, We Few

We Band of Brothers

by *Cindy Shanks*

We few, we few, we band of brothers
March on, our heads held high,
We who watched the flames scorch
New colours in the sky.

We few, we few, we band of brothers
March on, the music plays.
The screams of burning bodies
Will never die away

We few, we few, we band of brothers
March on, in living fear.
Fallen Ash, blistered hope.
Death dried up all our tears.

We few, we few we band of brothers
March on and on and on.
We few, we few we band of brothers
Leave one, by one, by one.

Stray Dog

Jude Fowler

Stray Dog

by *Jude Fowler*

SCENE 1 INT OFFICE DAY
(MANDY and SALMA are by the coffee machine)

MANDY
I was like, you were worried I might be
thinking – 'He's the one! That was so amazing
I want to marry him'?

SALMA
(snorts into her coffee)

MANDY
I was like, 'you're right. I am in love with
you; that was the most profound
experience I've ever had.'

SALMA
What did he say?

MANDY
Not a lot, just shuffled about looking
uncomfortable

SALMA
I'm not surprised. Bloody hell Mandy,
you're supposed to pretend a bit.

MANDY
Why? I'm sick of pretending.

SALMA
They're very sensitive about that

*(ANDREW walks through the open plan office. MANDY
& SALMA stop talking and watch him. MANDY heads
back to her desk and goes past ANDREW who is
behind a glass door she bangs on the glass and
mouths "I know you want me" ANDREW turns away)*

SCENE 2   INT   TRAM CARRIAGE   EVENING
*(VINCENT gets on, staggers through the carriage and
sits next to MANDY)*

VINCENT
People in here...just walked from
Scotland...shut up...bastards...can't
believe it...sorry love just need to sit down
for a bit...he's worse than he was.

MANDY
Who are you talking to?

VINCENT
I'll just stand over here, shall I?

VINCENT
(getting up, leaves his backpack)
We're at war, have you forgotten that?

MANDY *(follows him to door)*
Don't forget your bag

VINCENT

Sorry love I'll move it...Jesus Christ...
nobody can remember me...bastards...
shut up!

MANDY

How are you feeling?

VINCENT

I'm alright love; I'm alright, yeah alright

MANDY

Have you stopped taking your pills?

VINCENT

Don't need them; make me ill...shut up...
we're at war you know.

MANDY

You're scaring everyone

VINCENT

I'm not hurting anybody...I don't want to
hurt anybody...you want to go outside?

MANDY

We're on a train

VINCENT

Someone's nicked me baccy! Where you
going?

MANDY

This is my stop

VINCENT

Please don't leave me
(Doors open MANDY gets off)
You're the only one who cares

SCENE 3   INT.   SUPERMARKET   DAY
(MANDY is leaning over the frozen food section on her mobile)

MANDY

They haven't got any Mum...no; how about
cod in parsley sauce?
(MANDY looks up and sees VINCENT outside in the car park)
All right, I'll see ya later.

(MANDY watches VINCENT, he's animatedly in conversation with himself it makes MANDY laugh the girl on the checkout eyes MANDY suspiciously)

JULIE

You all right?

MANDY

Bet he's never lonely

JULIE

What...Do you want any help with your
packing?

MANDY

No.
(MANDY walks out leaving her shopping on the conveyer belt)

SCENE 4   EXT.   CANAL
(VINCENT is on a bench next to the lock gates. MANDY
approaches him and hands him a take-out coffee)

MANDY

Hello again

VINCENT

Cheers love

(There is a look that passes between them VINCENT
smiles, MANDY smiles back. VINCENT drinks his coffee
and they watch the ducks)

SCENE 5   INT.   OFFICE TOILETS
(SALMA and MANDY enter, SALMA goes into a cubicle.
MANDY leans against the sink deep in thought)

SALMA

It seems so sudden.

MANDY

I know...I think he's the one.

SALMA

Yeah I have come on, have you got one I
can borrow?
(MANDY pokes a Tampon under the partition)
Thank God for that. Last thing I need is
another baby.
(SALMA flushes loo, comes out and washes her
hands)

SALMA
Well he sounds really nice. When you two
get back off holiday you'll have to get him
to meet us after work one night, we can
all go out.
(dries her hands)
Remember to send us a postcard.

SCENE 6   EXT.   HIGH STREET   NIGHT
(MANDY and VINCENT are running down the
pedestrian precinct laughing, passersby look at
MANDY and move away quickly)

SCENE 7   INT.   MANDY'S FLAT   NIGHT
(MANDY and VINCENT are in bed, VINCENT is on his
side facing away from MANDY, MANDY is snuggled up
against him)

VINCENT
I can't; it's the pills.

MANDY
It doesn't matter.

(MANDY kisses the back of VINCENT'S neck, a tear
rolls over the bridge of VINCENT'S nose)

SCENE 8 INT. MANDY'S FLAT MORNING
BATHROOM
(MANDY is peeing onto a pregnancy testing strip – we watch the blue line develop VINCENT appears in the bathroom doorway)

MANDY
I'll have to get rid of it

(VINCENT kneels down on the bathroom floor MANDY is still on the toilet)

VINCENT
No! This is our baby. Our own Immaculate
Conception! We could call him Jesus.

MANDY
What if it's a girl?

VINCENT
I don't care. We'll be a great family. You,
me, a little girl called Jesus.

MANDY
You're mad

VINCENT
I know

MANDY *(tapping VINCENT'S temple)*
What have your mates in here got to say?

VINCENT
They're speechless...I love you.

SCENE 9   INT.   OFFICE   DAY
(SALMA is on the phone ANDREW is next to her looking concerned)

SALMA
You need to ring and let someone know what's going on.

SCENE 10   INT.   MANDY'S FLAT   SAME TIME
(MANDY is in her night dress, curtains closed, a blue light seeps into the room. She stands in the doorway listening to SALMA on the answer machine. MANDY looks ill – the blue light making her look pale, drawn and unwashed.)

SALMA (V.O)
Carol's going mad.
(Flash back to scene 1. Camera on ANDREW; MANDY comes up and bangs on glass. She mouths 'I know you want me' ANDREW turns away mouthing 'she's mad')

SALMA (V.O)
Where did you go anyway?
(During the rest of this speech we see snatches of scenes 2,3,4,6 & 7 but MANDY is actually alone. VINCENT doesn't exist except in MANDY'S head)

I don't even know if you're back yet. Are you sick? Just give us a ring or get what's his name to ring us. Can't wait to tell you what's been going on here while you've been away. Hope you've got a good tan. Call me when you get this message. Bye!

(MANDY turns away and goes to the bedroom. On the bedside cabinet is the pregnancy test with a clear blue line. MANDY gets into a messy bed and curls up against a pillow, she mumbles into it)

                    MANDY
I love you too.
                    (She smiles)

The Bag

Shura Price

The Bag

by *Shura Price*

"What's in the bag, jerk?"

He snatches at the strap across my body. Best not to speak. Words can provoke. Carrying a bag can provoke. Never mind the smile I had let slip this morning. He grabs the sleeve of my coat and shoves his angry mouth up close to my face.

"I said, what's in the fucking bag?"

His breath touches me. I can see his blackheads clustering round the rose pink flesh of a fresh zit. Just as his right arm pulls back to hit me, I hear my voice attempt 'books', the word mangled by the recently installed brace on my teeth.

"What the fuck you doing with bricks? You gonna throw 'em at us gayboy? No need to fear me. I ain't no racist scum. Give 'em here, I might slap your head between two and make a brick sandwich."

I'm trying really hard to repeat the word 'books' but he's not listening and the audience has arrived in the shape of his mate Tahir, a hefty mound of flesh with an ill matching square head. He squeezes my arm, hard, as a gesture of solidarity with Zitface.

"Gayboy's got a bag, and get this... it's full of bricks."

"Heavy, man."

"You hungry, Tahir? Fancy a sandwich?"

I can see he's hooked on the idea. But just as I am about to speak, Zitface starts pulling at the strap of my bag again; I think he really wants to rip my head off. For a moment I wish I had let my mum buy me a rucksack. At least that might have just dislocated my shoulders. I can hear her voice:

"Umar, listen to me, a rucksack is more sensible." When I had continued to resist she had played her trump card: "But everyone will call you gay with a bag like that."

Probably, I had thought, in the uncomfortable silence. I have to tell him it's not bricks, just books. Maybe he'll back off when I tell him, but before I get the chance, I'm tangled in the strap struggling on the floor, wondering whether it's worth getting a kicking to protect a few books. When they start to empty the bag there might be the chance to escape. But I underestimate Zitface's delegation skills.

"Tahir, you get him an' hold his arms, right, while I empty the bag."

Keen to demonstrate his commitment to the job, Tahir bear hugs me then tips me upside down and shakes me.

"What the shit! This ain't bricks, this is books, fucking books. What use is that as weapons? They ain't gonna hurt no-one."

That's not what my Dad thinks; he wanted to ban me reading 'Romeo and Juliet' at school until he heard all the other Dads were actually buying their kids copies of it because 'passing your exams is more important than worrying about a bit of a love story'. So now I've got to put up with reading about love sick Romeo distracted from his true love, Mercutio, by that oversexed Capulet girl. Zitface shouldn't underestimate the power of books.

Just in case I've forgotten who's boss, he kicks the pyramid of fresh new paperbacks scattering them across the muddy grass; for a moment he looks directly at me. Despite the thrill of fear, I have the sense to look away, just snatching a glimpse of the sharp blue in his eyes. He's sort of dancing around now arms punching, agitated, or maybe trying to fight off the invisible enemy.

This is when I expect to get kicked. Zitface isn't the kind of guy who deals well with disappointment and there's a cold wind blowing. His bare pink arms look mottled and lonely next to the white of his short sleeved school shirt. I feel sorry for him freezing his balls off, Mr Macho for an audience of two. Tahir's brutal grip crushes my moment of sentimentality and I remember that here, outside the school's perimeter fence, I'm far from help. Bloody stupid risk coming this way, I'm telling myself.

I nearly laugh with relief when Zitface picks up a book – Lord of the Flies. A rare sight: Zitface with a book in his hand. He's sort of weighing it. That's it. He's going to hit me with a book, test it out as a weapon. Thank god he didn't choose 'Lord of the Rings'. I wait, ready to ride the blow, but then I see that he is actually looking at the cover, which shows a fly infested, blood drenched head on a stick. Few ideas there for him. Thoughts of what he might do next turn my bowels to water, and I'm kind of thankful for Tahir's fearsome grip, otherwise I might slide boneless to the floor.

"What's this about then? Murder innit? You read this gayboy?"

"Nah.." and I don't make the mistake of smiling at him this time. I avoid his eyes and look to the distance where there's a great view of the cemetery.

"What about this one, Lord of the Rings? Should be good for a gayboy. So what's all this then? Homework? Bed time reading? Well I might have this one." And he stuffs 'Lord of the Flies' in his pocket.

"And this one, nice and thick, just for you, Tahir."
Zitface chucks the book, but Tahir doesn't loosen his grip on me, just deftly catches it one handed.

"What's this say then? Great Expiations. 'Ere that mad woman's in this, Miss Havisham. I remember, I sin the film in Miss Lomax's class. And that guy Magwatch, great guy, criminal, and there's this real good bit in the film at the end when Pip the little gay squirt…"

"Shut it!" By this time Zitface is so cold he can barely control his shivering so I figure either he'll leave or take revenge for his own personal and physical misery on me; thumping me would at least warm him up. Then his trusty sidekick, Tahir has a brainwave, not easy in a square head.

"'Ere, let's go an' get a coupla cans an' sit in the library. No staff there now, an it's nice an warm." He shoves me roughly to the ground, and the two of them, hands in pockets, march off, Zitface spitting over his shoulder, "You fucking fuck off – gay boy."

And that's it: cold and bored they're gone.

Phew, thank god no misguided do-gooding teachers came to rescue me; otherwise I'd have been in real trouble. So, in a way it was a good job I chose this devious way out of school to avoid the prying eyes of pretend friendly teachers on home time duty. I gather up my books and wipe off the worst of the dirt. When I get home I can easily clean the plastic covers with a cloth and a bit of washing up liquid. The hard part will be avoiding Mum's nosey questions. And I'll need a good story to explain away the mud stains on my coat otherwise she'll jump to the right conclusion; I can just hear her:

"I told you that bag would provoke people. I bet they called you gay!" She will barely be able to hide her satisfaction at being right. And it would only be a short step for her to say:

"You're not are you?!" Then we would have to have the 'big' conversation. This might not be a bad thing, but one confrontation a day is enough, even on my crazy personality building regime. Football, that's the answer. I'll tell her I was playing football with my mates. She'll get so annoyed about that, she won't be able to focus on anything else.

There's only two of my books missing; could have been worse. He might have trashed the lot, and then I'd have a guilty conscience for nothing. Someone should tell the librarian not to leave opened boxes of new books lying around before they've been stamped. Should make a bit of money on them at the car-boot sale on Sunday. Yasmin says they're classics and on the set book list at college. She's positive she can sell them. Then that'll be a bit more dosh to put towards a new mobile phone to replace the one I had nicked last week.

? Love

Sylvia Pryor

? Love

by *Sylvia Pryor*

Do you still love me?

How do you answer that,
looking into the eyes of someone
who was life itself to you,
who woke you from your hundred year sleep,
taught you to laugh and love then left?
For you there had been no more
love, laughter, light, dark or sleep, oh sleep!
Why can you not say at once
with a voice that could cut ice cubes
'Love you? – are you mad? – love you?'
But you can't.   Love still hides
in those treacherous eyes
as you know it does in your own.

Secret Code of Women

Madeleine Cullinane

Secret Code of Women

by *Madeleine Cullinane*

"But, Grandma, it hurts so much!" my childish voice wails.

"I know, sweetheart, and I'll finish the bindings as soon as I can," she says, kneeling at my feet, her grey head bowed over her task.

I can hear the tears in her voice but I can't feel their wetness, prevented by the thickness of the bandages she winds around my toes. The pain is all encompassing, excruciating. The other women must hold me down. My mother kneels, cradling my head on her green and red patterned lap, stroking my forehead. She's crying too, she knows worse pain is to come.

"Let's play a special singing game," says my Grandma.

So I begin to learn the nursery rhymes and songs. They are my introduction to the nushu, the secret code of women that has been passed down the generations. It was invented by my distant ancestor from the fertile Hunan province, who was taken as a royal concubine, in the time of the Song dynasty.

I am one of the sworn sisters who grow up together, offering each other support during the torture of foot binding, and re-binding, singing the ancient ballads to their soothing hypnotic melodies.

The custom is long established amongst the good families in our region, bound feet demonstrate a family's ability to raise a daughter correctly. A daughter is a drain on her father's purse until a socially suitable husband can be found, and tiny feet are essential for a good marriage, in order to please a husband sexually.

The sisters meet in a private sewing room, females only, learning the domestic way of life from our mothers and aunts. Sharing patterns and materials, working harmoniously together, we sing the stories as we weave, embroider and sew.

I start to learn the nushu, the secret language, and to recognise the thousand sounds of our special code. I learn to form the written words, making the shapes, wispy and rhombic, using the delicate strokes that are required.

With time I learn to improvise on the well known songs, and even to express my own thoughts in verse. Using the code I incorporate them into my needlework, disguised as a flock of distant birds in a sapphire blue sky.

"Oh Grandma, how will I manage?" I sob. "Separated from you and mother, and my sisters."

I've reached the marriageable age of thirteen. My feet have been remoulded into the desirable golden lotus shape, three inches in length. They meet with my future mother-in-law's approval, the dignity of her family will be maintained. Tomorrow I'm to be transported to my husband's family home, where my lack of mobility will ensure my purity, and my seclusion.

"You'll send us news," Grandma answers, "using the nushu"

So I communicate using the secret code, as the sisters have always done. I send messages disguised in embellishments on female artefacts, little gifts sent home to my relatives. My story is worked into the decorative borders of handkerchiefs, and news of the births and deaths of my children is painted onto silk fans. My relationship with my mother-in-law is told in coloured yarns woven into a length of brocade. These gifts are carried from one household to another, by unsuspecting men.

"I cannot allow my son's child, my granddaughter, to grow up with ugly big feet," says my mother-in-law. "Just like any peasant woman working in the paddy fields!"

But I have already passed one daughter over, to be initiated into the woman's world of beauty and pain, to have her feet broken and bound by the professional foot-binder engaged by mother-in-law. My child's screams, though muffled, could be heard throughout the house. Already she is walking with the painful tiny steps, the swaying lotus gait.

"You can't catch me, Grandmother," my spirited second daughter shouts. This strong willed and knowing four year old escapes from mother-in-law and runs out into the garden.

I take courage from her defiance, and add my determined voice, lobbying and persuading in the privacy of the marital bed. My husband takes a stand, defies his family, and so we prevail against the custom in our second girl's case.

I teach my daughters the nushu, we sing the songs as they practice their needlework. I show them how to write a message using embroidery stitches and silken yarn, representing seeds exploding from a puff-ball flower head.

My hair is almost white now, my eyesight is dim and my fingers too gnarled for handicrafts, my half finished work, a branch of white magnolia stitched on red silk, is laid on my lap. My first daughter is long dead and my second daughter is gone, married to a tribesman from a distant province.

When the time comes, it will be my remaining daughter's duty to communicate the news of my decease to her sister, and to my sisters at home. She is a sewing a pretty collar, incorporating a metallic silver thread.

I cannot foresee how many dynasties will rise and fall before the men in power ban the practise of foot binding by law, nor predict that the nushu will be lost and forgotten, suppressed during a cultural revolution. Perceived as grotesque novelties, the sisters' exquisitely embroidered tiny shoes will become museum pieces, Oriental antiques.

Summer Puppy

Alison Shelton

Summer Puppy

by *Alison Shelton*

You were a summer puppy
But in the autumn you found
That your oversized paws could carry you anywhere
You chased graceful deer
And leaping scolding squirrels
Or ran for the ear flapping joy of running.

You were a summer puppy
But in the autumn you found
That the treasures of the trees would fall at your feet.
With dinosaur bone sticks
And leaves to be leapt for
Kicked up high in an auburn confetti.

You were a summer puppy
But in the autumn colours change
And your face showed signs of silver as you ran
Over purple moorlands
And drank from laughing streams
Swelled with November rain and iced by the portent of winter.

You were a summer puppy
But in the autumn your breath
Would hang frosted in the air with mine
On nights of moonlit silver
Walking side by side, home
To flickering flames where rabbits were chased in doggy
dreams.

You were a summer puppy
But in the autumn we found
That as you shuffled beneath the oak trees
And looked to me
Then at the scattered piles
Your mischievous mind forgot your body's betrayal for a
moment.

You were a summer puppy
But this year I scoop
An autumn rainbow and let it fall, to see the laughter in
your eyes.
And we wrap your trusted blanket around
As the hearth holds no heat for you
Quietly resting with your head in my lap. You know.
I watch the fire die.

You were a summer puppy
But this fall I walk alone
And I will kick up the last leaves
As they drift downwards.
Just in case.

Silver Boots

Christine Holley

Silver Boots

by *Christine Holley*

Now, she really wanted a pair of silver boots, my partner that is. You know what women are like. Had to have silver boots with thin, very high heels for the office party, to go with her new dress. And she couldn't find any anywhere. I am a bit conventional in my dress myself – don't agree that clothes maketh a man - and didn't understand at all. She used to ask me about her clothes, but I never had anything to say, except that it was very expensive. I suggested e-bay for the boots. No - she didn't get on with e-bay, ended up with rubbish stuff that didn't fit and was the wrong colour.

So I said I would have a look. I actually rather like e-bay. You can buy anything, you know. So had a look while she was out with the girls. She went out a lot with the girls. Said I could go out with the lads if I wanted, but I didn't. Wasn't really into drinking competitions and laddish jokes. So I tended to stay at home and watch dvds with the cat. Ate noodles and chilli sauce.

I found some boots on eBay – silver, very high heels. How could anyone walk in those? And put in a bid. And won – congratulations, it said. Like it was a big achievement. Looked up the address and found it was Todmorden. Just down the road. Couldn't quite work out where but I suggested I collect and asked for an address and instructions. Received a very nice email saying that would be wonderful and how about that evening. I'm sure you're surprised to learn I found my silver boots in Todmorden, but it is not all free veg and marinas you know. There's a lot going on not even the Tod News can find out.

Well, to get back to the boots, I took the partner to the pub to meet her girlfriends, then switched on the sat-nav. I know – they can send you anywhere, but I was pretty sure I knew Tod and wouldn't end up perched on a rocky crag with no room to manoeuvre. Or stuck in a farmyard surrounded by cows and chickens.

Mind you my confidence did start to waver a bit as I drove up this steep road with a dead end sign on it, but I felt a lot better when I saw a pair of large hideously green gates at the end, left open for me as the email had said. I drove through them and there, just round the bend, this eerie, large house. I am rather fond of ghost stories and a few came into my mind as I wondered if this really was the place. There were bats dive bombing round it, owls hooting. But as I got nearer, the front door opened and I saw, framed by light from inside, this rather odd looking person. But with a lovely smile. I noticed the smile immediately. And delicious brown eyes. And a little dog yapping from behind.

Tight black leather jeans, loose white shirt. Fluffy red brown hair. The shirt was open enough for me to see a bit of curly chest hair. And he was wearing a pair of silver boots. The man, not the dog. Suddenly I rather liked silver boots.

Well, he asked me in. Said he had some cocoa keeping warm and cupcakes he had baked himself just that afternoon. Said there were too many for him and Percy. They were both watching their figures. Percy was the little dog by the way and didn't have enough figure to watch – he is no bigger than my cat. But I couldn't resist that smile and followed him into the house. On one side of the hall were a row of silver boots – I spotted one pair with my name on them.

Of course, I quickly told him that the boots were not for me. Felt I ought to put the picture straight from the beginning. He just laughed, said he could see that just by looking at me.

Wasn't too sure what he meant by that. We went into a room on the left – comfortable chairs, open fire, Bach playing on some snazzy equipment. I was never allowed to play Bach at home – girlfriend didn't like it – preferred Take That. I sat down and he brought in a tray with two large mugs of cocoa and some delicious looking little iced cupcakes. I was hungry. Only had a sandwich before I came out.

Percy sat down in front of the fire and Edwin, that was his name, curled up on the chair next to me. It was really cosy and nice. I took a sip of my cocoa and had a bite at a cupcake.

Now, something had an extra ingredient. I began to feel really relaxed and happy, then maudlin and sorry for myself, and under the influence of that kind smile I came out with stuff I didn't know I felt. How my girlfriend of eight years was never at home, always out with her friends. How my job was boring and I didn't think the alpha male boss liked me very much – kept making cracks about my clothes and the way I talked.

Edwin was very kind. He patted me on the arm and said he thought my clothes were absolutely right, and not everyone could be a macho male. He said he had had a partner but they had gone off only last month with an eBay customer – taking their silver boots but leaving no money. I vaguely wondered where all the silver boots came from.

By then I was not in a fit state to drive, I can tell you, and Edwin said I could stay the night. He showed me my room and said I could lock it from inside, just to show he had no intentions. He giggled when he said that and gave me a little hug. I slept very well, and didn't lock the door.

Next day I took the boots back home. My partner tried them on with her slinky dress and paraded up and down in front of me. I told her she couldn't walk in the boots and her tummy bulged at the front of the dress – well it did. But she shouted and slammed the door and stormed upstairs. I was only trying to stop her looking silly. After all, she wasn't a teenager any more.

So, things got a bit difficult at home. A lot of nights out with the girls for her. I ate a lot of noodles, and the cat went out every time I put the TV on. My job wasn't getting any better either. Started to feel a bit low.

Then I had a call from, guess who, bet you can't - Edwin. I must have given him my number, didn't remember but then didn't remember much else so wasn't that surprised. Did I like coq-au-vin? Was I doing anything that evening? The noodles went straight into the bin, the cat went into the cat box and we both went into the car. The coq-au-vin was delicious, and so was Edwin.

I never did go back. After a bit of yapping and a lot of hissing the cat established supremacy and harmony was restored.

Girlfriend's partner turned up one afternoon with some guy in tow. Edwin gave him the once over but decided to my relief he wasn't the right type. Feet far too big for silver boots and he looked like he thought he was in the wrong place. They just handed over various bits of clothes, cat food, Bach cds, packets of noodles and drove off looking rather bewildered.

No – I never wore silver boots – Edwin said they didn't suit me. Said he liked me the way I was. So I stuck with the sensible M&S brogues. We still sell them on eBay though – if you are interested.

Silver Boots

One For The Land

And Two For The Sea

Christine Potter

One For The Land

And Two For The Sea

by *Christine Potter*

One for the land and two for the sea

in darkness the tyranny
of the light is obvious
turning tripartite
first, a faint yellow in the sky
then a halo over the windbreak
then a flash
as the light does its duty
as beacons and lanterns have done
for sixteen centuries
One for the land and two for the sea

protecting mariners
from the graveyard of foul waters
nearly at the world's end
nothing more till Finisterre
(or Fitzroy – not nearly so final)
One for the land and two for the sea
One for the land and two for the sea
One for the land and two for ...

no letup
no safety in the dark
without the steady sweep of the light
endlessly rotating
One for the land and two for the sea

To My Darling Mary

Elizabeth McLaughlin

To My Darling Mary

by *Elizabeth McLaughlin*

"Come on, we've got to make a start", Jane turned wearily towards her brother Tom who was sitting disconsolately on the settee, hands hanging limply between his knees. "The longer we leave it, the worse it will be."

"I know", he responded. "It just seems so final. I don't like doing this."

"Neither do I, but it has to be done. We need to put the house on the market. It's been empty now for three months."

He sighed wearily and stood up. "All right then. Where do we start?"

"Well, I thought upstairs first. There are all her clothes and things. They need sorting and putting into bags for the charity shops. We can leave the furniture for the time being. The new people might want some things, especially if they are first time buyers."

Jane opened the door and they went up the familiar stairs. She fully understood her brother's reluctance. He was always the sensitive one of the family and he was very close to his mother. Her sudden death had hit him very hard and he was struggling to come to terms with it. It was only a year since Jenny, his wife had died and now this. Two deaths in such a short space of time had been a real blow to him. Jenny had been his soul mate and the discovery of the lump in her breast had been shocking as had the rapidity with which the cancer had spread to the rest of her body. Their mother had been the rock he had leaned on during that time and he missed her so much.

Jane pushed open the door. Their mother's bedroom was very traditional. A lovely old oak wardrobe with a mirror in the centre and a large drawer at the bottom, a chest of drawers and dressing table to match. It had been her pride and joy, always polished to a high shine and never a speck of dust to be seen.   There was still the vestige of the lavender polish in the air even though it was now nearly two months since her death.   On the dressing table were lots of photographs of the family at different stages of their lives and one of their mother's wedding.   Mum smiling proudly at the camera and Dad gazing at her with obvious love.

Jane picked up each one in turn and looked at it.

"Why did she have to go", Tom said.   "I thought she was perfectly healthy. I don't understand it."

"No, the doctors couldn't explain why she had the stroke. She didn't have any of the indications that they usually find. We'll never know. At least she didn't suffer. It was very quick."

"Let's get started", she said.   "You empty the drawers and put the newer looking things into one bag and the rest into another. I'll do the wardrobe."

He moved over to the tall boy and opened the top drawer. Jane watched him as he started to take out the gloves and scarves that were there. He placed them carefully on the bed in two separate piles. Satisfied, she turned towards the wardrobe and took a breath as she caught her reflection in the glass. It gave her quite a shock. The face looking back at her was almost her mother.   She shook herself and turned the little brass key in the lock.

A smell of mothballs wafted out.   All her mother's things were hanging neatly on good wooden hangers and arranged by type.   There were coats, blouses, skirts, dresses and surprisingly, a couple of pairs of trousers.   Jane had never seen her mother wearing pants.   She must have only worn them in the house when it was cold.   On the floor of the wardrobe were several pairs of shoes and handbags to go with them. Jane lifted out all the clothes, removed the hangers and laid them on the bed.   They were all in good condition and could go to the Charity Shop.   She was about to start folding them when a thought crossed her mind.   Her mother's every day handbag was there.   She reached into the dark depths of the wardrobe and took it out.   It was black leather with a flap over the front fastened by a strong magnetic stud.   She pulled it open and looked inside.

Her mother had always liked this bag.   It had lots of compartments which were very useful and made it easy to find things.   Jane had bought it her for a Christmas present about ten years ago. Inside were all the usual things, purse, comb, mirror, handkerchief, lipstick, powder compact, diary, pen and keys. There was a zipped pocket in the main compartment. Inside it was her mother's driving licence and a photograph. Jane pulled it out and looked at it. It was a small sepia photograph of a smiling man in army uniform. He was standing on his own in some place that must have been very sunny because his eyes were screwed up. When she looked carefully at the picture she could see that there were palm trees in the background and the front of a jeep. She turned it over. On the back were written the words "To my darling Mary. All my love"

"Tom, come and look at this photo, I have no idea who it is," she said.

He came and stood next to her and took the photograph in his hand. "It's definitely second world war," he mused. "No, I don't recognise him. It's certainly not Dad or Uncle Peter.

"I wonder if it was someone she met before Dad," said Jane. "She never talked about anyone before him though. He looks a nice man. Why did they split up?"

"Perhaps he was killed."

"That could explain why she has kept it in her handbag all these years. He must have meant a lot to her."

Jane took the photo from Tom and put it into her pocket.

"Let's finish sorting out these things and put them into bags. We can take them to the charity shop tomorrow," she said. "I think I am going to do some detective work and try and find out who this man is."

"How will you do that?" asked Tom, turning to look at her.

"Well, for a start, her best friend, Sheila is still alive and if anyone knows anything then she will. I'll go and see her on Saturday. You never know what we might find out."

Tom smiled. "This might be quite interesting. Let me know what you discover."

With that, they set to with renewed vigour and when they finally left the house laden with bags Jane was quietly pleased with the change in Tom's demeanour. This little mystery was just the thing to lift his depression.

"We'll see what tomorrow brings," said Jane as they closed the gate.

Surrounded

Janet Spooner

Surrounded

by *Janet Spooner*

"We've got yer surrounded!"
Julie Downie
Toughest kid at school
Cock of the North
Born a pit bull
With a fistful of razor blades
She'd sooner swallow
Than allow another to win
And a grin that could kill
From a thousand yards
Hard
Dead-hard
Steel-hard
Rock-hard
Diamond drill-hard

And your heart goes 'pit pat, pit pat, thud!'
And your blood courses through your ears
As the third years stare
The fourth years glare
The fifth years bare their teeth
And the sixth years couldn't give a toss
It's your loss
Cos they'd sooner touch tongues
Under the sultry sun
Behind the sports hall

"Shit fer brains!"
Julie Downie
Lip curled
Hurls abuse
"Look at your fucking shoes!"
Any excuse
To bring the lame, the brains
And the tosspots down
Concrete down
Oil slick puddle
Pretty rainbow
Down
Where you drown in sweet humiliation
To the jubilation
Of the gurning masses
And the rose-tinted glasses
Lie in shards
Around the high school yard

Where you now see
Needle-in-haystack
Sharp

And your legs go shiver, quiver, quake
And you make to leave, but she blocks the way
As the monkeys howl
The wolves prowl
Pitbull's breath spits foul
And the teachers raise their Guardians
Hide behind their cardigans
Cos they'd sooner find a cure for cancer
Than face the wrath of Downie

"We've got you fucking surrounded!"
Pitbull's hackles rise
Human shackles pull you forward
To Pitbull's yellow eyes
Size for size
You could mangle
Dismantle
This undersized cuboid of muscle
But you were brought up a nice girl
A good girl
A curl-in-the-middle-of-your-forehead girl
And when you were good
You were very, very good
And when you were bad
You were remorseful
So your eyes look down
To Pitbull's feet
Shoulders droop
Heart skips beat
And you wait for the pounding to come

And a voice says 'this is the way it must be'
And a voice says 'what is wrong with me?'
As fists pound
Slaps rain down
Claws grasp sheaths of hair
And the geeks turn and walk away
Around the corner to run away
Cos they'd sooner hide in shadows
Than incense the canine führer

Last Chance

Susan Silvester

Last Chance

by *Susan Silvester*

Chance Burnette smiled at Doctor Zeigler, his wounds beginning to heal. Zeigler had found him in the gutter a broken down compulsive gambler with the legacy of a losing streak and a debt repaid in broken bones and bruises. Zeigler had promised Helen her husband would be cured of his compulsion, which had left them both close to financial ruin.

Chance held the tickets for two to Vegas tightly in his hand; this trip would prove if Chance was cured, the doctor was bankrolling them to prove a point. Helen felt apprehensive as they headed towards the airport. They would take in a few shows, Zeigler said, Chance wouldn't go near a card table or a roulette wheel and she hoped he was right.

Soon they were in the dry Nevada heat speeding toward the Vegas strip. As they reached their destination Chance felt the compulsion to gamble getting stronger and stronger and demanded his half of the bank roll.

"Take it then," Helen barked. "Take the blasted money. We'll be on our way home in a couple of days when you've lost it all."

Burnette grasped the money, pushing his way through the crowd in the Lucky Strike Casino and made his way towards the blackjack table, as Helen disappeared in a huff in the opposite direction to see the Michael Buble show.

Easing himself into the plush red seat, Chance began to play blackjack and started to win a few hands. Although not winning every time probability seemed to be on his side. Two hours later Helen returned, quite expecting to see her husband stony-broke. As she entered her eyes were drawn to a large crowd surrounding the blackjack table.

"The guy's betting eight hands a time, all at the $2,000 table max," a tall thin man shrieked excitedly.

"And he's winning," another exclaimed.

Helen recognised her husband almost hidden by a mountain of various coloured chips. She grabbed a basket and began scooping the chips up and taking them to the payout counter, turning the chips into hard cash before her husband had the misfortune to lose everything yet again.

Much later a bleary-eyed Chance made his way to a fully comped hotel suite. The casino manager smiled slyly, he'd be back to lose it all eventually, he thought, shaking the gambler's hand. Back at their suite Helen urged Chance to take the money and run. The compulsive Burnette lay on the bed drowning in $100 bills.

"My head hurts," he said. "I keep seeing red and green lights and strange numbered equations in my mind."

Helen smiled. It didn't seem so bad now that Chance was a winner.

The next few days were just the same as the first. Continuous winning hands, pulling a huge crowd of admirers but this time the gambler noticed a couple of hard-looking men in black suits glaring across the table, making him feel nervous. The mean, ugly pair were Pit Bosses whose job it was to unnerve winning punters and make them leave. Still Burnette's compulsion demanded he play on.

A waitress with flowing blonde hair and a ready smile offered him a drink which Chance gladly accepted. Two or three hands later he began to feel woozy. Helen scooped up the chips while the pit bosses offered to look after her husband. Moments later the winning player found himself in a room flanked by the two heavies and staring in to the eyes of the steely eyed casino owner. A well manicured hand held a sheaf of tickets toward Chance.

"Take in a few shows, sir. Here are some complimentary tickets, but I urge you not to play blackjack in my casino again, though you're welcome to play any other game." His words rang with menace. One of the guys, smelling of cigars and heady aftershave who looked like a Rottweiler, spat out the words. "Remember, no blackjack here. We don't like card counters."

Chance was scared and blurted out the warning to Helen while she deftly counted the wad of dollars.

The couple slept in 'til midday but Chance still felt the urge to gamble. He'd try another casino, but word soon circulated and he couldn't get near a blackjack table. Walking over to the roulette wheel the atmosphere became less intense and the security guards relaxed.

Sitting down Burnette waited until the wheel had spun a few times. He felt an overwhelming urge to cover eight segments of the wheel over and over again and his instincts paid off. The eye in the sky continually watched as he amassed another quarter of a million, this time at roulette, another winning night. As Chance headed back to his suite a heavy blow cracked his head open, blood poured down his face. He was dragged into a dingy room and systematically stripped.

"Can't see a computer on him," one of the assailants said.

"Don't know how he does it. How does he cheat?" They threw him into a gutter where Helen found him.

"Better get out of Vegas," she said as her husband drifted in and out of consciousness.

Soon they were on the plane and Chance felt his compulsion to gamble dwindling away.

"It's ironic," he said. "When I was a loser everybody wanted me to gamble with them. Now I'm a winner I can't get a game, not even in Vegas." Chance never felt the urge to gamble again. Helen smiled, Hans Zeigler was right he had cured her husband and their money problems too.

Meanwhile Doctor Zeigler thought about when he was an MIT student majoring in artificial intelligence as well as medicine. Chance Burnette was the doctor's prototype, programmed with a master card counting formula to play perfect blackjack and with algorithms implanted in his brain to compute a winning strategy for roulette but only able to be activated in Vegas. By now Hands had many compulsive gamblers programmed and ready to go. Soon Vegas casinos would be brought to their knees, crumbling in the Nevada desert. Zeigler reflected on his time as a young rookie in Vegas with a few dollars and an idea for winning at gambling using pure skill. He got accused of cheating but now he had perfected a way of beating every gambling game known to man he would have his revenge.

The Contributors

The Contributors
in *alphabetical order*

Peter Baber

Peter can be seen in the most unlikely places around Todmorden. Climbing the Pike, diving deep underwater or savouring the tastes of Thailand. One thing you won't see him doing is writing, being a journalist and all.

John Clarke

John Clarke is from East London and moved to Todmorden in 2011. He is a graduate of the Young Writers Programme at the Royal Court Theatre which had a rehearsed reading of his play *In*. Other plays have appeared at Stratford Circus and his poetry has been published in magazines.

Madeleine Cullinane

Maddie is retired from a career in fashion, but the dress rail in her spare room still holds assorted theatrical costumes and a bridal gown awaiting alterations in its tell-tale white 'body bag'. She aspires to write historical fiction, incorporating romance and drama.

Jude Fowler

Jude grew up in Cornwall, did a pointless degree in Performance Art and earns a living from corporate role-play.

Years of bemoaning a lack of creativity led to her try writing. Now Jude is published in a book due out in 2012. She lives in Todmorden with a husband and 4 daughters.

Andy Fraser

Andy is trying out retirement at 40, if he likes it he may stay. Originally from the north of England, Andy's varied past can lead to him being mistaken for a 'southern ponce'. He lives in Todmorden with his wife, two cats and the largest collection of contentious opinions in the whole of the Western World.

Christine Holley

Christine has lived in Todmorden for 28 years. She enjoys eating, drinking and talking to the dog.

Richard Holley

Richard is a devoted follower of Lord Bacchus and divides his extensive free time between watching films, playing video games and reading books (as long as they have no practical application) as well as, of course, producing acerbic compositions for the writers' group.

Elizabeth McLaughlin

Liz is a retired primary school teacher who is now deeply involved with Todmorden Hippodrome Theatre where she designs the programmes for every production. Her hobbies include reading, painting, singing and trying to act.

Christine Potter

One of the founding members of the Todmorden Writers' Group and a published poet, Christine is active on many fronts around Calderdale – saving libraries and the labour party, publishing poetry anthologies, even leading her own writers' group in Burnley.

Shura Price

Shura writes as a hobby between reading and gardening. Poetry and the short story form interest her most for the challenge of compressing ideas into few words. The support and encouragement of the writers' group keeps her motivated and it's a pleasure to meet people who care to write. 'The Bag' was inspired by Shura's experience as a teacher (now retired).

Sylvia Pryor

Sylvia has been a member of the writers' group for over two years before which she was a published poet who performed her own work on Radio 4. Still, she doesn't blame the group.

Cindy Shanks

Cindy Shanks has been part of the Todmorden Writers' group since 2009 and enjoys the chance to meet up with other people who enjoy writing. She is a teacher and taught overseas for two years in Romania. She also enjoys travelling.

Alison Shelton

Alison has lived in Todmorden for five years and in addition to writing, she enjoys walking her dog up to Stoodley Pike; the moors being an inspiration for writing, and the Pike the subject of some poorly-skilled photography. Alison finds that she writes best when she lets the inspiration flow and doesn't edit; preferring to keep her pieces 'raw'.

Susan Silvester

Susan is a retired civil servant who has always lived in Todmorden. She loves reading, walking and knitting. Susan really enjoys the challenges and feedback that the writing group offers.

Janet Spooner

The Lesser-spotted Spooner hibernates through the long northern Autumn, resurfacing only when the Christmas Holidays begin. Janet has been a professional writer, performer and director, though now she prefers to teach.

Photographs:
The Pike in Mist taken by Alison Shelton
White Tree taken by Jude Fowler
Cover photo and image jiggery-pokery by Andy Fraser

www.ingramcontent.com/pod-product-compliance
Lightning Source LLC
Chambersburg PA
CBHW072358190626
46811CB00019B/1394